leapfrog

Bill's Baggy Trousers

First published in 2000 by
Franklin Watts
96 Leonard Street
London
EC2A 4XD

Franklin Watts Australia
14 Mars Road
Lane Cove
NSW 2066

A CIP catalogue record for this book is available
from the British Library.

ISBN 0 7496 3709 9

Series Editor: Louise John
Series Advisor: Dr Barrie Wade
Series Designer: Jason Anscomb

Printed in Hong Kong

Bill's Baggy Trousers

by Susan Gates

Illustrated by Anni Axworthy

W

FRANKLIN WATTS
NEW YORK•LONDON•SYDNEY

Bill's mum bought him some new trousers.

The trousers were very big and baggy.

They had lots of pockets.

Bill's mum sent him to the shops.

"I can put the shopping in my pockets," said Bill.

"I'd like some potatoes, please," said Bill to the shopkeeper.

The shopkeeper helped
Bill fill his pockets with
the potatoes.

"I can't walk!" said Bill.

14

"My trousers are much too heavy."

Bill took all the potatoes
out of his pockets.

Suddenly, the wind began
to blow up Bill's trousers.

They got bigger and
bigger and bigger.

"Oh no!" shouted Bill.
"I'm floating away!"

Bill floated high up into the sky.

He floated over the town ...

... and waved to his mum in the garden.

Bill's mum didn't see him.

"Look at me, Mum!"
shouted Bill.

Suddenly, a bird pecked
Bill's trousers.

They went Sssssssssss ...

Bill's trousers got smaller and smaller.

"Look out! I'm coming down," he shouted.

Bill landed next to his mum in the garden.

"You were quick!" she said.

Leapfrog has been specially designed to fit the requirements of the National Literacy Strategy. It offers real books for beginning readers by top authors and illustrators.

There are five other humorous stories to choose from:

The Bossy Cockerel   ISBN 0 7946 3708 0

Written by **Margaret Nash**, illustrated by **Elisabeth Moseng**

A traditional farmyard story with a twist. Charlie the Cockerel is very bossy indeed. The hens think it's time he got his come-uppance ...

The Cheeky Monkey   ISBN 0 7496 3710 2

Written by **Anne Cassidy**, illustrated by **Lisa Smith**

A hilarious story about a little girl with a vivid imagination who encounters a monkey hiding in her treehouse. Read all about the exploits of Wendy as she tries to make the mischievous monkey leave.

Mr Spotty's Potty   ISBN 0 7496 3711 0

Written by **Hilary Robinson**, illustrated by **Peter Utton**

A rhyming text with repetitive and patterned language about Mr Spotty's attempts to grow seeds in an old potty. It soon becomes clear that Dot, his dog, may be the reason behind his success.

Little Joe's Big Race   ISBN 0 7496 3712 9

Written by **Andy Blackford**, illustrated by **Tim Archbold**

An outrageously silly story about the adventures of Little Joe as he runs an egg and spoon race that turns out to be more of an experience than he bargained for!

The Little Star   ISBN 0 7496 3713 7

Written by **Deborah Nash**, illustrated by **Richard Morgan**

A fantasy story with an element of humour about a little star who no longer wants to live in the sky. His friend, the Moon, takes him on a magical journey to show him how much fun the sky can be.